Dear Parent:

Congratulations! Your child is taking the first steps on an exciting journey. The destination? Independent reading!

STEP INTO READING® will help your child get there. The program offers books at five levels that accompany children from their first attempts at reading to reading success. Each step includes fun stories, fiction and nonfiction, and colorful art. There are also Step into Reading Sticker Books, Step into Reading Math Readers, Step into Reading Write-In Readers, Step into Reading Phonics Readers, and Step into Reading Phonics First Steps! Boxed Sets—a complete literacy program with something to interest every child.

Learning to Read, Step by Step!

Ready to Read   Preschool–Kindergarten
• big type and easy words • rhyme and rhythm • picture clues
For children who know the alphabet and are eager to begin reading.

Reading with Help   Preschool–Grade 1
• basic vocabulary • short sentences • simple stories
For children who recognize familiar words and sound out new words with help.

Reading on Your Own   Grades 1–3
• engaging characters • easy-to-follow plots • popular topics
For children who are ready to read on their own.

Reading Paragraphs   Grades 2–3
• challenging vocabulary • short paragraphs • exciting stories
For newly independent readers who read simple sentences with confidence.

Ready for Chapters   Grades 2–4
• chapters • longer paragraphs • full-color art
For children who want to take the plunge into chapter books but still like colorful pictures.

STEP INTO READING® is designed to give every child a successful reading experience. The grade levels are only guides. Children can progress through the steps at their own speed, developing confidence in their reading, no matter what their grade.

Remember, a lifetime love of reading starts with a single step!

For Chip, Julie, and Benjamin.
A special thanks to Shana Corey
for putting my pumpkins in order.
—C.G.

In memory of my mother, Dorothy Spengler.
—K.S.

www.stepintoreading.com

Educators and librarians, for a variety of teaching tools, visit us at
www.randomhouse.com/teachers

Library of Congress Cataloging-in-Publication Data
Ghigna, Charles.
Oh my, pumpkin pie! / by Charles Ghigna ; illustrated by Kenneth Spengler. — 1st ed.
   p.   cm. — (Step into reading. Step 2)
SUMMARY: Rhyming text describes the different shapes and sizes of various pumpkins and notes what they might become—including pies, scarecrow heads, and jack-o'-lanterns—once they leave the patch.
ISBN 0-375-82945-8 (trade) — ISBN 0-375-92945-2 (lib. bdg.)
[1. Pumpkin—Fiction.   2. Stories in rhyme.]
I. Spengler, Kenneth, ill. II. Title. III. Series.
PZ8.3.G345Oh 2005   [E]—dc22   2004012608

Printed in the United States of America   20 19 18 17 16 15 14 13 12 11
First Edition

Oh My, Pumpkin Pie!

by Charles Ghigna

illustrated by Kenneth Spengler

Random House 🏠 New York

Autumn in the
pumpkin patch.
No two pumpkins
ever match!

See them growing
row by row.
Pumpkins put on
quite a show!

Pumpkins come
in many sizes.
Pumpkin shapes
are such surprises!

Pumpkins round
as basketballs.

Pumpkins flat
as old beach balls.

Pumpkins striped

in shades of yellow.

One looks like
a large marshmallow!

Some have bumps.
Some have none.

Some look like

a setting sun.

Some look like
a big balloon.

Some look like

a harvest moon.

Some look like

a spinning toy.

Some look like
a baby boy!

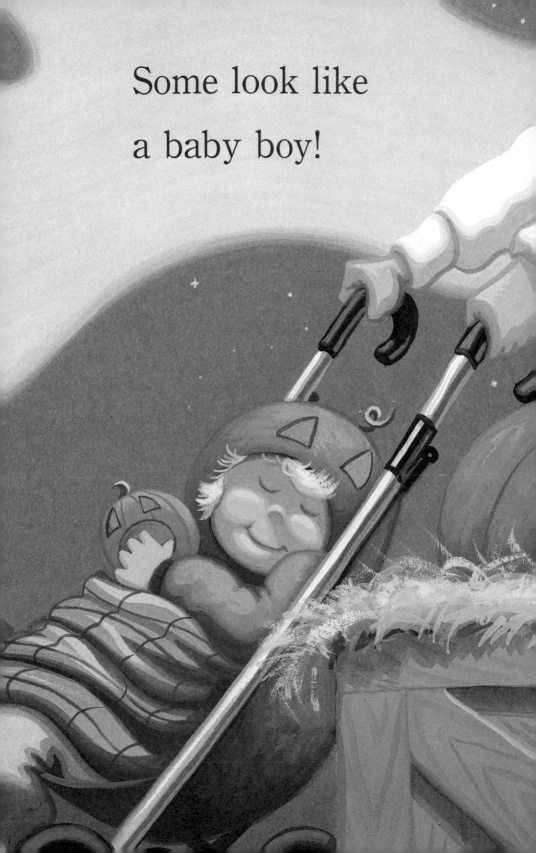

Pumpkins skinny.

Pumpkins fat.

Some look like
a tabby cat!

Some are shaped
just like a pear.

Some go to
the county fair!

Some BIG pumpkins
win a prize.

Some wind up
in pumpkin pies!

Pumpkin muffins!
Pumpkin bread!

One becomes

a scarecrow's head!

Pumpkin butter

on your toast.

Pumpkin seeds
are fun to roast!

What's the biggest
one you've seen?
Was it during
Halloween?

Looking friendly?

Looking mean?

With a smile

or with a scream!

Pumpkin faces
burning bright
in the cool
October night.